Lost
Ralia

GEOFFREY GAY

Ark House Press
PO Box 1722, Port Orchard, WA 98366 USA
PO Box 1321, Mona Vale NSW 1660 Australia
PO Box 318 334, West Harbour, Auckland 0661 New Zealand
arkhousepress.com

Unless otherwise stated, all Scriptures are taken from the New Living Translation (Holy Bible. New Living Translation copyright© 1996, 2004, 2007, 2013 by Tyndale House Foundation. Used by permission of Tyndale House Publishers Inc., Carol Stream, Illinois 60188. All rights reserved.)

Some names and identifying details have been changed to protect the privacy of individuals.

Cataloguing in Publication Data:
Title: Lost Ralia
ISBN: 978-0-6487150-3-0
Subjects: Fiction; Poetry
Other Authors/Contributors: Gay, Geoffrey

Design by initiateagency.com

CHRONICLED BY THE KING'S SCRIBE

~ Friar Raymund of Ruthaglenn ~

Translated and brought to Public Attention by

~Geoffrey Gay ~

For my dear wife, Jill,

and our very own

Daughters of Eve and

Sons of Adam[1]: Sarah and

Renee, John and Jason

And in memory of my Great

Great Grandfather, William Gay of

Ballaarat, Poet Extraordinaire!

HEAR YE ! HEAR YE !

BE IT KNOWN FROM THIS DAY FORTH that the events recalled in these published annals may not relate to events as they may have happened in the past, may be happening presently or may happen in the future in this land; that all persons involved in some large or small role in these published annals may not correspond to present or past characters on this continent, or may not be a reflection upon any personal traits residing in its inhabitants; that the nature of people and places, whether for the light or darkness, is in no way an allusion to present standards or conditions – one hopes!

GG

With the deepest regard and heartfelt affection for
the traditional custodians of Gondwana East.

Map

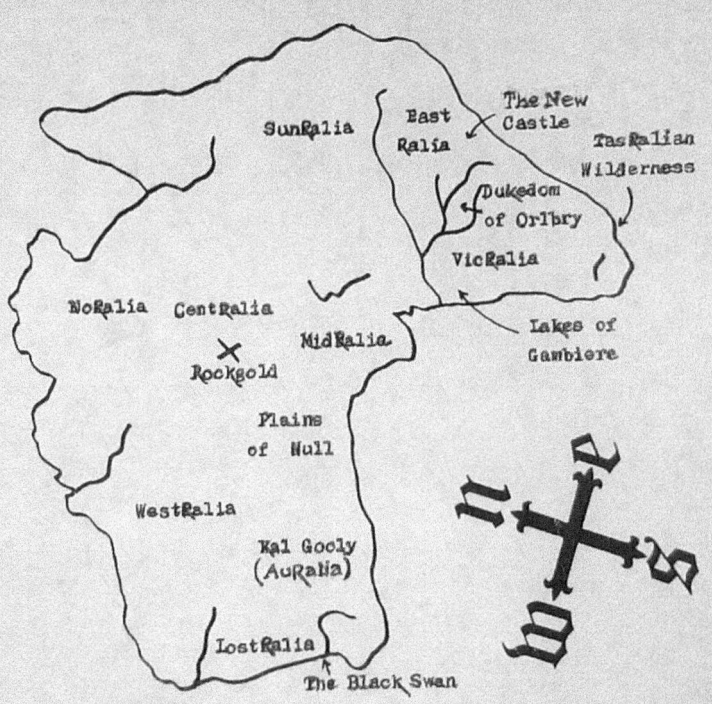

SunRalia
East Ralia
The New Castle
TasRalian Wilderness
Dukedom of Orlbry
VicRalia
NoRalia
CentRalia
✗
Rockgold
MidRalia
Lakes of Gambiere
Plains of Hull
WestRalia
Kal Gooly (AuRalia)
LostRalia
The Black Swan

AND the LORD GOD
said,

Behold, the man is become as one of us,
to know good and evil:

and now, lest he put forth his hand, and take also
of the tree of life, and eat, and live forever:

Therefore...

Genesis 3 : 22, 23

SCROLL THE FIRST

THE YEAR: In the mists of medieval time...

THE BANQUET HALL IN THE NEW CASTLE ~
the demesne of Prince Cavaliere, Lord Designate of EastRalia:

Wherein Cavaliere and Sir Sedny plot their
strategy to thwart the designs of the
Devious Sir Ben Deego of VicRalia.

"O Sedny, my Dearest Knight,
Why do you slurp your food?
Place your giblets on the dish
And please do not be rude!

"There is a matter that I have
That is of great import.
If you will hearken to my words
I'll tell you of the sport."

A pregnant pause did follow;
'Twas the Prince Cavaliere,
Who stole his knight's attention
With a keen intensive stare.

"Before the morrow's dead and gone
Ben Deego you'll have slain.
Your lance and sword will have been used
To bring to us great fame.

"He comes to us in vengeance,
Vendettas to secure
A foothold in this kingdom,
With power and wealth our lure.

"An enemy so dark and dim
He has proved to be;
But when you Sedny slay the man,
The honour rests on me."

"My Sturdy Prince, I do perceive
That you are full of light.
With such an enemy as this,
I'd rather that YOU fight!"

"My Daring Knight, why do you doubt
That you can do him in?
To fear that he's too good for you
Is verily a sin.

"The continent of Ralia
Can only e'er be wronged,
If Deego is allowed to breathe –
His wretched life prolonged.

"So give yourself to chivalry
And everything that's noble,
For if you do there is no doubt
Our fame will soon be global.

"MidRalia, also, must be saved,
We cannot be afraid;
I'll give my life to such a quest
And court Dear Adelade.

"O Adelade, the Fairest One,
O how I love thee truly!
Your treasures are the richest
And your gold is from Kal Gooly.

"I seek to wed Dear Adelade.
She MUST be my wife.
Either save this Lady Fair
Or give her up to strife!

"That scoundrel Purth is after her
To steal her hand from mine.
If we can soon be rid of him,
That will do me fine."

"Cavaliere, er, prithee please,
Why this Dark One Purth?
Methought it was Ben Deego
That's causing all this dearth."

"My Knight, you are mistaken,
It's not like that at all.
Ben Deego's just the lackey -
It's Purth that stands so tall.

"Let me tell you of this rogue.
Sit back and hear the tale,
That you may stand against him too
And cause the fiend to fail.

"It was so many years ago
When forebears sought new lands,
Sailing o'er northern seas
To walk these golden sands.

"Some moved into NorRalia,
Some moved into the south,
And others to VicRalia,
We know by word of mouth.

"Most settled in EastRalia
But many have forgotten,
How they worked to bring forth fruit –
Now by some made rotten.

"In time the prophets screamed abroad:
"A king shall lead us on!"
Cavaliere the Elder rose –
His leadership waxed strong.

"Not all men were bent on this,
One snake held out with greed –
Name: Manzana Putrida;
Avarice: his only creed.

"For countless years he made his plans
Then rode off in the night.
He took with him some ruffians
All looking for a fight.

"He pillaged and he burned his way
Across the Ralian slopes.
Bloodthirsty was his cohort –
He taught them all the ropes.

"With cruelty and torture
He ravaged all the south;
Making slaves of natives,
With cursings in his mouth.

"But worst of all he took with him
The dearest one of all.
My father now is lost to us...
Righteous hearts did fall.

"A boy was I, I could not see
How I could rescue him.
Years have passed and hopes are gone;
The memory's growing dim.

"There is no proof that he is dead.
I cannot bear to think
Of stories that brave men do tell;
I doubt there is a link.

"They say he rots in bondage,
Of that I can't be sure.
A symbol of our impotence;
I desire to do much more.

"But that does not seem urgent now
As I relate to you,
This shameful tale about a man
With his shamefully vicious crew.

"To the west he rode on now
Across the Ralian plain,
To foster his new empire;
The man was far from sane.

"And now he claims a castle,
Aptly named: 'Black Swan';
His sobriquet: The Dark One Purth;
His mission: Out to con.

"He always dwells in darkness,
Planning all the day.
He schemes to have Dear Adelade
And put her right away.

"And if that ever happens,
The continent will suffer.
Adelade dwells in the south –
We need her as a buffer.

"He now has others in his thrall,
For many has he bought;
Lord Melbun has succumbed of late
To rally round his court.

"And then there is Ben Deego
Underneath his spell;
Working as *charge d'affaires* –
The whole affair doth smell!

"I do not know about the north,
Perhaps it will survive;
I pray for Princess Alice
That she'll keep our hopes alive!

"For all I know that's all he has
To aid him in his quest.
There is much more for me to learn -
He'll put us to the test.

"Rest ye now, Sir Sedny,
There are matters on my mind.
Rest this night, Sir Sedny,
For strength that you must find."

Pipers' tunes flowed through the hall,
Distinctively required.
The music was as soothing balm -
The melody admired.

The banquet hall grew drowsy
For night was closing round.
Sir Sedny rose to take his rest;
To jousting he was bound.

Cavaliere, the troubled prince,
Rose from his troubled throne.
He could not help but feeling
To ill-fortune he was prone.

But now he must have courage
To meet the deadly foe.
Although that peril nears him,
To bed he now must go.

SCROLL THE SECOND

The next morning on New Castle Common:
Wherein the Champion, Sedny,
is challenged by Deego upon the jousting field;
And Cavaliere is confronted by a further mystery...

Red, blue, green and gold,
Blowing in the breeze;
The flags waved welcome to the knights
Who hailed from other leas.

Cavaliere, our Noble Prince,
Stood in all his splendor.
A quickening light shone from his face -
Life he must engender.

On his steed sat Sedny,
Plumpest of the knights;
Although he felt quite nervous,
He longed to reach the heights.

"Sedny, Sedny, Faultless Knight,
Are you waxing brave?
This day you fight Ben Deego –
Such a naughty knave!"

"My Dearest Prince, you are so great
To sponsor such a quest.
I feel the blood run through my veins;
I hope to do my best!"

"My Knight, please think upon this deed
That forces us to fight.
There is so much at stake here,
As we discussed last night.

"Although Ben Deego comes today
To wrest our honour from us,
I fear there's much more danger here...
I've been a Doubting Thomas.

"Last night I stirred upon my bed,
Woken by a thought.
I found it hard to comprehend –
Finality it brought.

"As Ben Deego fights today
Our thoughts are turned t'wards him,
Remembering not yon Purth's foul schemes
And his part in this sin.

"I wondered why there was a need
For Deego's presence here.
DISTRACTION, yea, the sickening plan –
That is what I fear!

"The Dark One Purth knows what I want;
He is such a cur!
Whilst we're disposed to fight this joust,
He rides and snatches HER!"

As Cavaliere prepared to move
Away from Sedny's horse,
A knight stepped out in front of him –
A 'fearsome-looking force'.[2]

Ben Deego's shield flashed in the sun;
Cavaliere stood still.
Ben Deego's frame quite menacing,
With looks to surely kill.

"So here you are Ben Deego,
Your presence long-awaited;
Arriving under cover to
This rendezvous ill-fated."

"Cavaliere, I fail to see
How you can save your life,
Let alone ride to the West
To save your 'trothed wife.

"Many moons will pass from now,
My cunning Purth has planned;
You shall never reach her
Across this endless land."

"Ben Deego, your tongue is forked.
I do not trust you – ever!
My love shall one day reach her;
Your Purth is not so clever.

"But I perceive upon your shield
A symbol of great fame?
Tell me now, Ben Deego,
Its power and its name."

"Ha ha! Your curiosity
Is finally aroused.
This power that resides with Purth
Is binding your espoused."

"But what has that to do with this
That rests upon your shield?
The secret that is bound in it –
The secret that is sealed."

"Touché again, my Foolish Prince,
Do you think I'm stupid?
I've not come to play your games;
To waft around like Cupid!

"For you to find the mystery
That is to me so nigh,
One will have to joust with me –
I will have to die!

"Seek you out, Cavaliere,
A champion that's meet,
And I shall knock his block off
Underneath my feet!"

Cavaliere, unperturbed,
Called upon his knight.
Sir Sedny donned his helmet –
His body shook with fright!

Their trusty steeds pranced to the mark
Where both stayed 'ere they go.
They need muster all their strength
To withstand every blow.

Lifting up a bright green flag,
The Prince appeared to pray;
He held the flag above his head
To bring down as he may.

Swiftly now the green came down
And sent them to their fate.
The crowd rose with expectancy
And quaked with dreaded hate.

Crashing 'gainst the lances,
Blood began to flow!
But each man kept his station
To strike another blow.

They wheeled upon their horses
And swords came rushing out,
To smite each other's torsos
And end the bloodied bout.

Sedny strove with shouting
Whilst wielding all his force,
And smashed the blade against the knight –
It took him off his horse!

Ben Deego stumbled on his knee;
His armour weighed a ton.
Sedny seized this very chance
And sensed the victory won.

"I don't believe my fortune!
I haven't yet been dropped.
If I can stay upon my nag,
My head cannot be lopped!"

Sedny's blade screamed through the air,
Whistling from a height,
And swung towards Ben Deego;
It gave the fiend a fright.

The edge just caught the helmet
Above the culprit's ear.
It forced him to the ground again;
His end drew very near.

One final swing came from the knight
That struggled on the ground.
Yet all his energy was spent;
No fight could now be found.

The anxious Sedny raised his sword
And brought it swiftly down.
No movement from Ben Deego –
Death clothed him in its gown.

A roar came from EastRalians!
The wicked sod was dead.
Cavaliere stood upright
And lifted up his head.

Silence fell upon the throng;
The Prince began to speak:
"Ben Deego's death is timely –
Life's favours to the meek.

"But this affair continues
And I shall not be pleased,
Until I have Dear Adelade –
For then am I appeased."

A messenger pushed through the crowd
And strode towards the throne.
He bowed and begged an audience,
Then came a saddening groan.

"O Gracious One, I do perceive
That victory here is yours.
Yet if you do not hasten,
You will lose your cause.

"The Ralian Grand Duke Orlbry
Seeks to have you there,
To share with you strange tidings;
This Duke indeed does care."

"I shall rally forces
And travel to your land.
Time is very precious –
I'll join him hand in hand."

Cavaliere took off his cloak
And moved onto the field;
Reaching o'er the dead man,
He took the blood – stained shield.

Its symbol glistened in the sun –
Its power was to bind.
Cavaliere retained it –
The secret now to find.

SCROLL THE THIRD

That same day on the Road to Goolwar Shore in MidRalia:
Wherein the Lady Adelade retreats to
Goolwar Shore to escape the universal conflict
that is brewing,
only to find that mischief is closer than she thinks...

A kangaroo bounced from the path,
A dusty bumpy way,
That led towards the ocean
On a hot and steamy day.

A caravan moved silently
Under shady trees.
Bound was Lady Adelade
For airy wide blue seas.

Her car was borne by courtiers,
Noble ones by birth –
Loyal to their Lady
Through any sort of dearth.

They looked upon their Lady
With wonder and delight.
To look upon THIS Lady
Was a grand and pleasant sight.

With her sat her nephew,
A sprightly little chap.
He was occupied with mastering
A secret ancient map.

This parchment found amongst the jewels
In Adelade's abode.
Its outlines and its ancient runes
Revealed a secret code.

Yet Adelade's dreams rest elsewhere,
Straying t'wards her Lord.
This mighty Prince Cavaliere –
In no way was HE flawed!

Then from her mouth came flowing words,
Firm yet rather soft;
Enough to grant command to those
Who carried her aloft.

"Halt there, My Folk, I do believe
That it is time to rest.
When we arrive at Goolwar Shore,
I wish to feel my best.

"Although we go to holiday
Along the foamy coast,
We cannot let this journey harm
What benefits us most.

"The affairs of state do weary me,
Let's hasten to exclude
The tension that's been brewing –
A continental feud.

"So now I shall have sleep, My Folk,
Please halt! It must be done.
Then place me 'neath a eucalypt
Out from the noonday sun."

A bright young man with great wide eyes,
Being full of grave concern,
Sought to change his Lady's mind
And stop this brief sojourn.

"Dear Lady, if I may but speak,
Your poor and humble squire.
I would not camp along this way –
The danger seemeth dire."

Adelade peered down at him,
His prayers to her behove,
But his dear Lady's mind was fixed;
She motioned them to move.

Her carriers and courtiers
Sped off into the grass,
Off the road some fifty yards
Should something dangerous pass.

They placed her car beneath a tree
That stood beside a creek.
Her subjects moved away from her,
A resting place to seek.

That keen young squire did wait with her;
He lay just near her feet,
And slowly went to sleep right there –
He could not fight the heat.

The guards and nobles dreary now,
Their heads and shoulders dropped.
The animals retreating;
The birds' gay songs had stopped.

All was silent 'neath the trees;
An eerie atmosphere.
And then a danger unforeseen
Drew very, very near.

A rider came within earshot
And then rode close inbound;
Dismounting from his thoroughbred
He shrank behind a mound.

Then slowly on his feet he moved
From tree to bush to shade;
He kept his eyes upon the car
That held fair Adelade.

Dressed in grey and robed in black,
His cruel face wore a snear.
Intentions rather obvious
He slunk within her sphere.

Without a sound he kept his feet,
Onward he did strive.
Silence now his one concern
To take his catch alive.

No one stirred beneath the sun;
A sticky, sweaty hell.
All lay still along the road,
Captured by the spell.

The horseman now had reached her car,
He stopped and peered around;
Then fixed his eyes upon the prey,
Yon trees made not a sound.

Moments passed, his eyes did stare:
Cold and hard and bleak.
He took one step towards the car
As if he were to speak.

The curtains round the car hung still;
White with frilly lace.
He drew the fabric with his hand
And looked upon her face.

Her eyes met his, and his likewise
Both locked into a stare.
He sought to nullify her mind,
Bound in his mental lair.

In trancelike state, without a doubt
Her eyelids ceased to blink.
She couldn't see a thing at all;
Her consciousness did sink.

Adelade's young nephew,
Slumped upon his seat,
Had dropped his map beside her,
Underneath his feet.

This second prize the rascal saw
As he surveyed the scene:
"A map, forsooth; that must be it!
An extra treat to glean."

The spalpeen bent his bulky frame
And took it in his hand,
Then placed his arms 'neath Adelade,
The Fairest in the Land.

Quickly now he took her from
The sleepy company.
The eeriness remained with them;
Not one of them did see.

And then he flung her on his steed,
Her being still entranced.
The rider wheeled the beast around;
The Dark One Purth will dance!

Off along the way he rode;
Off into the deep.
The animals and the birds dead still;
The courtiers asleep.

SCROLL THE FOURTH

Two weeks hence in the Domicile of the Duchy of
Orlbry, in the southern reaches of EastRalia:
Wherein the Grand Duke Orlbry confers with
Prince Cavaliere on the whereabouts of
a missing wise man;
also to learn of more heartbreaking news from the west...

"Alas, My Dear Cavaliere,
Prince of this great land,
My heart at once goes out to you
Desiring Adelade's hand."

The Ralian Grand Duke Orlbry
Sat opposite his friend,
To form a plan of battle;
This awful rift to mend.

Orlbry now continued
To reveal his troubled mind,
"Allow me please to share with you,
If you will be so kind.

"I've heard a tale about a man:
A miserable, stricken wretch.
A man of wisdom years ago -
A man that we must fetch.

"He does not live but just exists;
Cave-ridden, old and worn,
Imprisoned in those fiery depths;
His countenance forlorn.

"Together we must rescue him,
I've heard he holds the key
To news that may unfold for us
If we're to jump with glee."

Cavaliere, holding back,
Decided now to speak:
"Please tell me, Grand Duke Orlbry,
Why *this* man you seek?

"I wish to face the Dark One:
That fiend who is so slick,
Not to tour infernal depths
For one that may be sick."

"My Lord, My Lord, do not arrive
At ill-conceived conclusions,
I always keep myself away
From devilish illusions.

"You see, My Liege, this one did suffer
Many years ago;
Our charming Purth – that dirty dog –
Counted him as foe.

"And then this wretch came under siege
To this carnivorous sinner,
Who threw him 'neath the Dreaded Lakes
For Cror to claim as dinner!"

"Alas, Dear Orlbry, what's it mean,
This Cror beneath a Lake?
Is there such a monster?
A drink, for Courage' Sake!"

"A monster? No, Cavaliere,
For Cror is far from that;
One musn't say it's ugly,
Slimy, green or fat.

"But mark my words, Cavaliere,
One cannot see this Thing:
This phantom, O so deadly;
So few escape its sting!

"Time is of the essence,
I daren't tell you more;
But we need save this victim,
From the wicked claws of Cror!"

A shadow crept across the brow
Of Prince Cavaliere;
There had to be a purpose
That the Grand Duke should now share.

Orlbry's face was somber,
Grim and grave and tragic.
Some answers lay within the mouth
That spake of evil magic.

"Our victim knows the secrets
That I believe you seek.
Apparently the news escaped;
There has been a leak."

"Who is this man? What is his name?
Pray tell, what does he know?
How does he relate to us?
Can he slay our foe?"

Orlbry gazed upon his liege,
With eyes both blank and grey:
"We must seek out this bod, My Lord,
Whilst we draw breath this day."

At once the door flung open,
As if struck by a gale;
A miserable boy came staggering in,
With an equally miserable tale.

The candles' flames did flicker,
And the atmosphere waned cold,
As this dirty, trembling youngster
Came forward to greet the Bold.

Accompanied by the sentries,
The lad seemed rather small;
His dress stamped him as noble,
Though his eyes and mouth did fall.

"Excuse me, Lords, I just rode in,
I do not bring reports;
That make your hearts sing gladly,
But will only bring retorts."

"Halt! Stand there this instant!"
Cavaliere marched thither:
"We do not even know your name...
This is no time to dither!"

"Forgive me, Lord, I do not crave
To mock your etiquette;
The news I have may break your heart,
Although we've only met."

"Speak up then, Lad, do not be shy.
We do not mean to bite.
Present these tidings to our ears,
Speak up with all your might."

The boy glanced 'round the chamber,
His nerves were sure to crack.
Although some tears rolled down his cheeks,
He straightened up his back.

"My name is Noah Lunga
And Adelade is my aunt.
I know you wish to win her hand;
Now I'm afraid you can't."

The story then unfolded
And the ghastly details given.
Cavaliere stood stony still;
His heart was near to riven.

"O Adelade, Dear Adelade,
My rage is surely swollen!
A vicious crime against this land
To think that you've been stolen!"

His eyes met Orlbry's and he knew
All hope was nearly lost.
But his dear Lady must be found;
Redeemed at any cost!

"The map! That map!" cried Orlbry;
A sudden fear rushed in.
"The theft of it reiterates
The raft of this great sin.

"Purth has gained this treasure,
This boon that he has won;
The map holds many secrets
Underneath the sun.

"It behoves us now to action:
Swift and sure this day,
Before that rogue finds knowledge
That will blow us far away!"

Cavaliere looked puzzled
As Orlbry spilled the beans:
"The map that Noah Lunga lost
Is full of nasty scenes.

"Underneath the Golden Rock,
Above MidRalia's plains,
Sit hordes of buried coffers
That may contain our banes.

Fiery swords and shields with force
And stacks of hidden jewels,
Pose a threat if found too soon
By overzealous fools.

"If this Purth possesses
All the power that he will need,
Let us act now quickly!
Before he makes us bleed.

"That wretch below the Dreaded Lakes
Of whom I spoke before,
Must now be sought with liveliness;
He surely knows the score."

"Your fears do not surprise me,"
Said Cavaliere, now maimed.
"For both of us there is a quest;
Much good may then be gained.

"I have a plan that will suffice;
This setback we shall block.
You will seek those deadly banes
Beneath the Golden Rock."

"And what of you, My Noble Liege?
I hope not what I think.
Hasten you to Gambiere?
Destroy our vital link?"

"It must be done!" the Prince exclaimed,
"We have no other choice.
When I shall return to you,
Then we shall rejoice.

"Learning secrets from this one
Who knows more than we do,
Only then can we chase Purth,
And stick to him like glue.

"Orlbry, GO! Do not be moved
By plans that make one frightened.
Do your duty for the realm;
Our vision must be brightened.

"We'll meet again, not long from now
And weld our knowledge surely.
It will be best to join our forces
Just outside Kal Gooly."

With that both men departed,
To seek what they most hunger.
Cavaliere called forth his force;
With him rode Noah Lunga.

Intriguing notes concerning

SCROLL THE FIFTH

IT IS WITH GREAT REGRET...

I announce that the long-awaited fifth scroll, concerning the annals of Ralia and dating from _____, has not as yet been recovered from the archaeological sites.

The others, of course, have been unearthed from the Primitive Monastic Library at Strumlov Mount in the region now known as the Australian Capital Territory.

Many scholars of world renown agree that the fifth scroll presents a detailed and active portrayal of the dangerous journey of Cavaliere's company from the Grand Duchy of Orlbry, touching the northern extremes of the TasRalian wilderness, leading to the Dreaded Lakes of Gambiere in the south-eastern reaches of MidRalia.

Excavation is still in progress, with scholars hoping for an immediate breakthrough. However, the publishing of what is available to us must not be delayed any further.

Please digest the remaining scrolls and be enlightened with the unfolding of its contents.

GG.

SCROLL THE SIXTH

A month of days hence at the Blue Lakes of
Gambiere in the eastern reaches of MidRalia:
Wherein Cavaliere seeks out the missing wise man,
whilst encountering another sinister barrier to their plans...

The stench and smoke rose upwards,
Fouling breathing air;
Covering the old volcano
'Round the Lakes of Gambiere.

Brave riders galloped down the slopes
That led to tragic fate.
Cavaliere and Sedny stopped
Outside a bolted gate.

"How are we to penetrate
This barrier of steel?"
Sir Sedny asked of his dear Liege;
Great tensions all did feel.

"To reach beyond this metal block
Would aid us in our quest,
Unless there is another way
That leads to our grim test."

There was indeed, as they soon learned
From local, loyal scouts;
Deep caves along the southern ridge
Removing nagging doubts.

No guards stood there to keep the maże
From foreigners and foe.
All too scared to near the Lakes
That told of unsung woe.

As Cavaliere descended
With Noah Lunga and his knight,
The atmosphere waxed thicker;
Their lungs contracting tight.

"Fear doth live in this abode,
We'll conquer it with faith,
And find our quarry still alive;
We must believe he's safe.

Cavaliere pushed on until
The darkness took them over;
When suddenly a light they saw
Above their heads did hover.

"Rather strange," they all surmised,
"It doesn't feel evil."
All followed it for quite some time,
Down to a lower level.

It danced and played above them
And begged them to persist.
At last they reached their destiny –
The Brave One clenched his fist.

He slammed it on his palm as he
Behoved the stricken wretch,
Surrounded in this cavern,
With chains that made him stretch.

The bearded man reached out a hand,
All but skin and bones.
He spoke with lucid clarity
In rather captive tones.

"My Son, Dear Son! It's true, you're here;
My light did seek you out.
Remove these chains and you will see;
Believe me, there's no doubt!"

"My what? Dear Man, I do not know
What all of this can mean.
Why do you claim that I'm your son?
You...I've never seen!"

"It is a shame, the years have passed;
Times have gotten bad.
Cavaliere, My Son, Dear Son,
Recognize your Dad!"

Cavaliere peered closely through
The dim and coloured light:
"My grief, it's true! How can it be?
I've suffered such a fright!"

"Many years have come and gone,
I gave you up for dead.
Yet here you lay before my eyes
With grey upon your head!"

Tears did flow between the two
As time stood still forever,
Until a roll of thunder crashed
Their newly-found endeavour.

"What is that?" Sir Sedny cried;
He quickly drew his knife.
"Verily not a storm out there;
On that I'll bet my life!"

"It's as I saw," the King now warned,
"The enemy draws near.
The evil thing that Purth has loosed
Would fill us all with fear.

"But that's its only weapon,
So don't despair – be brave!
And let's escape from this dark hole
That's been to me a grave.

"For countless years the *hoi polloi*
Have counted me as dead,
Yet Light will ever shine from Me,
So get you here," he said.

Cavaliere the Younger turned
Upon those rusty chains,
That had held his father hamstrung,
Providing many strains.

He smashed away the fetters
And lifted King so sore.
Sir Sedny and Noah Lunga searched
For detours 'round yon Cror.

Through a tunnel, onto a ledge
And out into a chamber;
A golden glow, pulsating light
Now greeted them in amber.

"Cror is here...I feel it!"
Cried Cavaliere the Old,
"Walk with haste and do not fear;
All this day be bold!"

Young Noah Lunga shivered
As he crept towards the glow,
And Sedny's sweat rolled down his cheeks;
He'd never felt so low.

"Sedny, keep your heart, My Champ;
Don't succumb, My Friend.
This thing is but a powerless trap;
Your mind it wants to bend."

The hapless knight lurched forward,
His hand clutched o'er his heart,
As if he'd been the victim
Of a swift and fiery dart.

The Elder King released a cry,
Both urgently and strong:
"Flee now Fear! It's time you go;
You have no right to wrong!"

At once the fitful knight collapsed,
He seemed to twist and flip;
And with one loud despairing shriek,
Delivered from its grip.

Forsooth, the chamber brightened;
Clear light shone in once more.
All could easily see the way,
Sir Sed rose from the floor.

"I'm alright now, although I've been
From here to hell and back.
Please let me thank you for your words
That made up for my lack."

"No time for conversation now,"
The old man wisely spoke,
"We have to find the exit soon,
And doubt we must revoke."

Quickly now the party moved
Into another tunnel,
Ascending to a deeper vault
That looked just like a funnel.

And at its top an opening showed
The sky both blue and grey.
Crusaders gazed with eager eyes;
God's Speed! They need to pray.

Up they climbed with grasping hands,
Up and through the hole.
Minutes passed, at last they reached
Their tiring, well-earned goal.

Thunder roared beneath their feet;
Cror was unimpressed,
That they had overcome its power
To press on with their quest.

"Now much haste is needed,"
The young prince made aware,
And led his fellows down a slope
Beside blue Gambiere.

Kal Gooly still awaits them,
A rendezvous to keep
With Orlbry and his secrets,
That for this while do sleep.

SCROLL THE SEVENTH

Many days hence at the foot of RockGold[3], in CentRalia:
Wherein Orlbry confronts
the 'Rat in the monolith's shadow,
only to be confronted with a sickening sight that delays
him in his fulfilment of the original plans...

The thump, thump, thump of horses' hooves
Betrayed the riders' speed,
As Orlbry raced across the plains
To RockGold's hidden creed.

Many days it took his troops
To forge their way inland,
When finally out of nowhere
Rose the Rock that is so grand.

Natives fled, the dingoes howled;
Their urgent message brought
An eeriness so desperate...
Hope almost come to nought.

The monolith leered down upon
The troops as they dismounted.
Orlbry searched along its base;
Stealth was now what counted.

Around a wall and through a passage,
Orlbry led the way,
Until he came upon a sight
That kept his troops at bay.

Gathered in the distance,
About one hundred yards,
Soldiers sat around a fire,
Playing a round of cards.

Orlbry viewed beyond them
A single black-cloaked rider,
Laying down beside his mount,
Gulping potent cider.

Glistening in the fire's glow
A Shield caught Orlbry's eye;
Tucked away behind the mob
That was to them so nigh.

"Don't tell me we've been beaten
In this grave and deadly race!
We must attempt to grab that Shield;
Put flight to our disgrace."

Before he'd finished speaking,
A blood-curdling, fearful howl
Echoed from above them;
'Twas enough to turn one's bowel.

A guard had spotted Orlbry's troop
And raised the shock alarms.
Then from the camp the scoundrels raced
With swords poised in their palms.

Paralysed from head to toe,
Orlbry's men did groan;
That darkest menace, Fear, had gripped
Our heroes to the bone.

With a rush the brigands fell
Upon the Duke and Co,
And took them all as captives;
Their hearts were full of woe.

"So what is this, My Lovelies?
A motley-looking bunch!"
The rider cursed with drunken breath:
"Indeed I have a hunch.

"Methinks you've come to spy on us
To see if we're connected
In any way to Adelade;
We hear that she's defected!"

Bent in two with laughter,
The rascals jeered and mocked.
The private joke they all had shared,
But Orlbry's mirth was blocked.

"Let me introduce myself,"
The rider bowed down low,
"I'm named Sir Bell a'Rat by most;
To you I'm just the foe.

"I have your dear, dear Lady,
And refuse to give her back.
To think that you could reach her now;
Do you think I'm slack?"

"So you're the one...mine enemy!"
Orlbry's tone did show
His desperate plight at such a time;
What a bitter blow!

"Yes, I am he whom you despise;
The one that got away
With that gorgeous prize, fine Adelade...
We have her here this day.

"But not for long, for I have planned
To send her far from here;
That will give you time to think
And time for you to fear."

Sir Bell a'Rat then sauntered
With his vermin and his prey,
Returning to the fire
Where the mystery Shield now lay.

In the glow it shimmered
With a strange compelling light;
Orlbry now saw clearly
Whence the Dark One sought his might.

"So now you have the fateful Shield;
We did not know you'd gain
Such a strange and potent symbol,
That is to most a bane."

The Duke of Orlbry's words betrayed
A note of grave despair.
He knew what Bell a'Rat had planned;
The truth was now laid bare.

"So now we know you used the map
To bring you to this place,
And whisk away this blessed scourge;
Its symbol on yon face."

Orlbry's men were kicked and shoved
And forced to bite the dust.
Sir Bell a'Rat took up the Shield;
Not ever prone to rust.

Its green background stood out somewhat
In contrast to the sand,
And on it glowed a Golden Tree,
Unusual to this land.

"ARBOR VITAE, Holy Saints!
Your cunning will suffice
To place us all in danger
If you carry out this vice!"

Orlbry choked upon his words;
He knew all hope had fled.
Sir Bell a'Rat just leered at him
And flicked away his head.

"I'm sure you realize Purth's power;
I hope it makes you quake.
My Duke, your liege's Adelade...
Mere icing on the cake!"

"What do you mean? Come here you cur!"
Screamed Orlbry from the ground,
"Is this another trick of yours?"
His head began to pound.

The errant knight gave orders
And his cohort jumped to please.
They bound their captives' hands and feet
And propped them on their knees.

"That should keep you quiet for now.
We'll take your weapons from you.
You need not follow us at all;
The sun will set upon you."

He turned away from Orlbry
And leapt upon his horse.
"Bring them out!" he shouted,
"We must follow this night's course."

Out from a hidden cleft there lurched
A sorry gang of slaves.
They looked as if they'd spent their lives
Beneath Earth's deepest caves.

Most of them were natives,
Easy prey to those
Slothful, hardened pillagers;
Enslaving as they chose.

Following upon their heels,
A sad, heart-breaking sight...
Dear Adelade, still in a trance;
Her eyes perceived not light.

The rider sat astride his horse;
The 'Rat beheld the prize,
And lifted her upon his mount
Despite dear Orlbry's cries.

"Farewell, You Filth, I hope you burn
Upon these desert seas.
Now try to follow us tonight -
Crawling on your knees!

"Our slaves we need to aid us through
These parched and desert places.
Doubt that you'll have anyone
To guide your pallid faces."

With that they moved into the dusk,
Their speed increased with time;
Racing o'er the desert plains
To hasten Purth's foul crime.

Meanwhile the Duke of Orlbry knelt
And prayed for quick release.
His men were waxing restless;
They hoped this trial would cease.

Many hours had passed that night,
Full moon had risen high;
When suddenly from on the Rock,
A loud, but subtle cry.

Some natives moved down quickly
From their vantage point so near,
And slunk towards the captives;
They had nothing now to fear.

The bonds were loosed and all concerned
Could not contain their joy,
As the Duke beseeched their rescuers
To partner his employ.

Gathering some booty
That Sir Bell a'Rat had left;
Available to Orlbry's troops
To counteract the theft.

Finally the deal was struck,
And though much time had gone,
Sir Bell a'Rat must not escape;
The desperate chase was on!

SCROLL THE EIGHTH

Weeks and days hence upon the Plains of Null
in the western reaches of MidRalia:
Wherein Cavaliere and his Liegelord thunder towards WestRalia
to hunt their infernal prey, and to unravel certain mysteries
concerning the Shields...

The desert sun beat ruthlessly
Upon the Plains of Null,
As riders galloped urgently
On past a rotting skull.

Cavaliere the Younger's mount
Was steadfast in its speed,
For the time was drawing closer now
To smash the Dark One's deed!

The rescue of his father
Was to all a timely tonic,
For the situation called for one
Whose terms were quite draconic.

A lifetime seemed to pass them by
As they rode on and on.
Their plans were bandied back and forth,
Yet none looked fit to don.

An oasis loomed up finally
To relieve both bod and brain;
At U-kla Well, did seem the place
To rid their hearts of strain.

The expedition pulled up hence
Beside a clump of trees;
A chance for tiring lords and squires
To pray on bended knees.

Cavaliere showed weariness
Upon his tested brow;
Concentrating keenly
On Dear Adelade and his vow.

"Our time is brief, My Father,
We must put forth a plot,
To rid this land of evil force...
To rid us of this blot!"

Cavaliere the Elder leaned
Against an old gnarled root;
Noah Lunga couldn't wait to take
A pebble from his boot.

"Peace, be still, My Troubled Son,
Do not allow the storms
Of anger and frustration
To invade in all its forms.

"Believe, My Son, it is your strength.
Nothing can destroy
Our faith, our hope, our courage
In the plan that we deploy.

"My memory now does shed a light
Upon a fact or two.
Methinks poor Orlbry's gone adrift...
He lacks the vital clue.

"Perceive do I in my Spirit's Eye
A slimy, black-cloaked rider,
And your Sweet One upon his mount;
Our plot is for to find her.

"Orlbry's now not far behind,
Additions to his party.
Haste and feeling not enough;
He dare not be foolhardy."

"What else is there that you perceive?
What can we now expect?
The Younger's Eye with growing strength
Like the One who can detect.

"A basic truth is near you, Son,
A truth where all must yield.
A pattern now quite obvious
Is latent on your Shield.

"Sir Bell a'Rat has in his hand
More than your heart's treasure.
A Shield of great import is his;
By this *your* Shield can measure."

"You say there's two of what I have?"
The younger lord was puzzled,
"From Deego confiscated
When he at last was muzzled."

"That's true, My son, the mystery clears.
Now look, what do you see?
What images revealed to you
From that lively silver tree?"

Indeed this tree of silver
Against a brazen hue,
As if the symbol pictured
A scene endowed with dew.

And scattered on its branches,
Contrasting in their sight,
The fruit of many actions –
Some dim and some that's bright.

"Dim and bright upon a tree?
Dear Father, what's it mean?
How is this of import?
Why *this* hazy scene?"

The Elder's gaze was steady,
Though his general features wild:
"There's no ken of Dim or Bright,
Proclaim the Truth, My Child.

"Bright, the image of what's good,
Reminding you of right.
Dim, to indicate the wrong,
Blind as moonless night.

"And BOTH these shades do dance within
Your weak and 'mortal coil'⁴.
A symbol of your nature;
How they sweat and fight and toil!

"A Tree of Good and Evil –
Symbolic Day and Night,
Of Positives and Negatives,
Of KNOWING Wrong and Right.

"Now this bane is in your grasp,
And this shall surely maim us.
Yet Bell a'Rat does hold the key
And by it does constrain us.

"The Shield that he possesses now
Is similar to yours.
A sacred, fruitful, Golden Tree:
'Tis made of different Laws.

"The Tree of Life, a tree of grace,
Regardless of your stations,
The extension of God's Fountain
For the Healing of the Nations.

"The Tree of Life to set you free
From Death and its foul sting,
From Good and Evil, Dim and Bright –
The Tree to which YOU cling."

Cavaliere, Noah Lunga
And the courtiers sitting by,
Enthralled by revelation
As the day began to die.

The Younger spoke up freely,
For all was not quite clear:
"If Bell a'Rat now has this Shield,
How deep must be our fear?"

The Elder lifted up his head,
His countenance was stern:
"Listen now, My Son and Heir.
Hear and you will learn.

"'Tis obvious Purth learned the clue
From Bree the King by name.
SunRalians did hide the Shield
That now is called Bree's Bane.

"From there it was quite simple
For the sod to snatch the Shield,
To undertake his evil plan
And gain all power to wield.

"Manzana Putrida knows full well
What trouble can be wrought,
If both are placed TOGETHER
In his dark and dingy court.

"The Tree of Life if added to
The Tree of Good and Evil,
Will multiply Eternal Death –
Divisive in upheaval.

"The Knowledge held within both
Shields – Infinite the tolls.
Free access to both the Trees
Not meant for mortal souls.

"The bait, My Son, is Adelade
To lure the big fish in;
Wanting YOU, this Shield as well,
To birth his final sin.

"When Bell a'Rat delivers both
Into his crafty hand,
Darkness reigns forever
Across this open land!

"Ralia can be lost, My Folk,
If we are not alert.
We'll cut Sir Bell a'Rat well off...
God's might and power assert!

"Prevent him. Don't be weak, My Son;
Keep the Shield at bay.
Establish it upon thy oath.
Your faith will save the day."

"But if I have the Tree of Death,"
The Younger drew him nigh,
"To rid the land of this one scourge...
I shall have to die!

"The Evil One will want to kill
Whoever has this Shield.
To win the one that he'll soon have -
I must humbly yield.

"And if I am a sacrifice
To save the Shield of Life,
Then how can I reach Adelade
And gain her as my wife?"

The Elder's eyes lit up with joy,
And then he wryly said:
"Repossess the Tree of Life,
And you're no longer dead!

"But now I'm speaking mysteries,
Not all will understand
Until these deeds do come to pass –
Your time shall be at hand."

They searched beyond each other's eyes,
The Truth was seeping through;
Yet their courtiers quickly waning
For their sleep was overdue.

Early on the morrow
They would ride into the West,
And make amends where'er they could
With nothing but their best.

This trysting time of great import
Would surely seal their fate,
Unless of course Sir Bell a'Rat
Reserves another date.

Down to sleep the courtiers sank;
Sir Sedny and the rest.
Noah Lunga and Cavaliere prayed
To pass the fiery test.

SCROLL THE NINTH

Several days hence near the wild mining township of Kal Gooly;
Wherein an expected confrontation is engaged and
much blood is shed, albeit what is sought requires
further seeking...

Lightning thundered in the heavens,
Foretaste of the danger;
A greeting to familiar beings,
A warning to the stranger.

As Bell a'Rat rode into view,
Kal Gooly lay before him.
The natives cowered and spat his name,
All sought to plain ignore him.

And tagging on behind him,
Like soaked and matted dags,
His cronies fought to keep their mounts
With loot stacked in their bags.

Adelade, bewitched and still,
Upon the bounder's gelding;
Her presence lame and powerless
To stall the Shields' melding.

All dismounted with their pillion,
Pitching damp and mildew tents;
Bell a'Rat now ever watchful
In rain and atmosphere so dense.

'Twas now a chance to drop the load
Relieve their aching bones;
Awaiting further orders
Amidst reluctant groans.

Time now weighed most heavily
Upon this ragged troop.
Time to plan their strategy,
To cheat, to trick, to dupe.

So that all's not lost too soon,
They must protect the bounty.
Bell a'Rat at length resolved
To send her from the county.

And of this Shield, named King Bree's Bane,
That seeks to grant one Life,
It must be hidden from the One
Who seeks his future wife.

Bell a'Rat with foresight vowed
To send her forth with some,
Then face the confrontation
That tactically must come.

Having thus accomplished this,
He set himself to wait
For Cavaliere the Younger,
Who was sure to take the bait.

Days and nights crawled slowly;
Gloom fell on every face,
As patience grew unwillingly
In that God-forsaken place.

Cavaliere, now pounding in
Towards Kal Gooly's field,
Held close to him the deadly curse:
That silver tree-bound Shield.

His troops and courtiers aware
Of hidden, hostile spies,
Overseeing their swift approach
Amidst the steam and flies.

Finally this day had come
When deadly foes would meet
Upon the battlefields of gold,
With spark and fire and heat.

Cavaliere the Elder then
Held up one bony hand,
And halted the crusaders
To hear his stern command.

"My People, hearken to your King,
The enemy knows we near
The trap of their contrivance;
It is plain to any seer.

"'Tis obvious, dear Orlbry Duke
Shall not arrive in time,
So I have now devised a plan
To counteract Purth's crime.

"We split in three, an hundred each⁵,
And wait till blackest night,
Among the heaps, away from eyes
That seek to sap our might.

"Then as the enemy slumbers
Upon his drunken bed,
A horn will sound the battlecry
As if to wake the dead.

"Swiftly then with torches lit
And swords and cudgels drawn,
Descend the heaps and smite the foe:
New champions – be born!

"Now heed my warning, Young and Old,
Regard the Golden Tree.
Let no harm befall it –
It must return to me.

"Go, My Folk, and heed your Prince,
For he must bear the brunt
Of swordsmanship and combat
In this keen and sombre hunt."

As Sedny turned his mount around
To organize his men,
An arrow sped into the dust
Not far from yonder fen.

The startled troop looked to the source,
Screamed Sedny unperturbed:
"A warning shot – not meant to kill –
Pray, be not disturbed!"

"Methinks 'tis more than just a shot
To warn of foul intent,"
The Elder King approached the knight
With head and shoulders bent.

"This goad that points towards the sky
Is aimed to spur us on,
Into nearby battlefield
To front the 'Rat head on.

"But we shall not be party
To his repugnant schemes;
Take no heed of Bell a'Rat
And his deceptive dreams."

With that Sir Sedny gave the nod,
And took his troops beyond
A mound that overlooked the camp,
Hard by a swampy pond.

The others too now disappeared
Into some barrow cores,
Awaiting dusk and darkness
That descend like eagles' claws.

A skirmish here, a melee there
The spies were active still,
To lure the troopers into war –
Secure the easy kill!

Yet Cavaliere the Younger,
He would have no bar of it;
He made short work of each of them
And sent them to the Pit.

By now the 'Rat was puzzled
As to why no news came forth,
With no sight of rival warriors
From east, west, south or north.

Suspicion overtook his calm
As he began to pace,
And consternation overtook
His usually cunning face.

Ordering more guards to watch
The entrance to their site,
The 'Rat was wary of attack
Sometime into the night.

He then retreated to his tent
To drink away his trial;
Not even sleep or wanton dreams
Could wash away the guile.

Hours passed and nothing stirred
Beneath the crescent moon.
The fen-fires flickered in the light –
Portents of the doom.

Suddenly from nigh about
The sleeping, lying dogs,
A trumpet blasted clearly
Through the early morning fogs.

Torches flamed and voices rose
In triumph with the lamps,
And warriors raced fearlessly
Down slopes toward the camps.

Sir Bell a'Rat awoke with fright
As he began to hear,
Doom descending swiftly
From surrounding heaps so near.

His guards were racing madly
From right to left and back,
Screaming curses wildly;
Seeking foes to hack.

With confusion quickly setting in
Among the vermin hoard,
Imagination rampant...
Alarmed in one accord.

Thinking there were thousands
Upon gold-mining hills,
The rogues now in a frenzy
Went pale around the gills.

And shimmering in the swampy bogs
The fen-fires lent their aid
To melt their weak hearts further...
Their glow did wax, then fade.

"Cavaliere! He rides with ghouls!"
They screamed into the night;
"Will-o'-the-wisps and spectres!"
They cried and shook with fright!

Not knowing who to counter,
Not knowing which was which,
They fought and scratched and bit and crawled
And fell into a ditch.

Swords went flying left and right,
Not one of them took cover;
Driven by an unseen power,
They began to slay each other!

Souls were lost and life was spent
Upon this gruesome night;
And not one prayer accompanied them –
Eternity a plight!

Before Cavaliere and friends
Could reach them from the mounds,
The carnage and the slaughter ceased
Amid blood-curdling sounds.

His troops and he were staggered
By the mess now at their feet;
Not one could take the credit
For this massacre complete.

All had perished, but our Liege
Pressed forward out of sight;
Administer the *coup de grace*
On Bell a 'Rat the knight!

SCROLL THE TENTH

The tragic scene of the campsite:
Wherein discoveries are made and further
plans are devised... And then,
A few day's journey from destiny's end
in the far western shoreline region of WestRalia:
Wherein Cavaliere and his entourage
forge ahead in their approach
to a risky encounter...

Once inside the campsite,
They searched till hearts were flat;
No sign of Lady Adelade...
No sign of Bell a 'Rat.

Signifying danger,
Their absence caused a scare;
'Twas obvious Sir Bell a 'Rat
Had sought another lair.

Amidst the goods and chattels,
The corpses and the mire,
The Shield of Life could not be traced...
Another loss so dire!

Having pulled apart the camp,
Retrieving nothing known;
Again crusaders far too late...
Many chances blown.

Far away the Lady
And the Golden Tree embossed;
Cavaliere and company
Were laggards double-crossed!

Noah Lunga loudly sobbing,
Alone and in despair;
Vengeance welling in his soul,
Though powerless to dare.

"Where is her deliverance
From this unending trial?
Is she to die in hopelessness?"
He spat the words with bile.

"No, My Lad, do not be cursed
With bitterness so sharp."
The Elder once again came forth,
Yet had no wish to harp.

"Success springs from a clarity
Of heart and mind and will.
This mission is not meant to feed
A sick desire to kill.

"Yet we must move with lightning speed
If we're to save the hour.
Upon thy horses – now!
Dear Men, Sally forth in power!

"Westward, further westward,
The 'Black Swan' now awaits
This King's arrival from afar,
Complete with all its baits.

"No time to wait for Orlbry,
We know not what they do.
'Tis sure he shan't be very late
When we upset the *coup*."

Off they sped towards the sea
To find the true solution;
The rising sun behind the troop,
Before them dread pollution.

For many days and nights they strove
Into WestRalia's lands,
Lost into a fatal webb
By Purth's corrosive hands.

Relentlessly they pushed and coaxed
Each tired and weary frame;
The very land itself began
Its work to halt and maim.

The seering orb above their heads
Beat mercilessly, 'twas sure
That every man upon his mount
Felt sickened to the core.

And finally, with knowledge bought,
From serfs and local cranks,
The warriors resolved to camp
Along Swan River's banks.

Not far from where they pitched their camp,
Now less than one day's ride;
Beyond the hills, before the surf –
Cavaliere's Sweet Bride.

Morning forced its way upon
The stiffened, yawning troops;
With plans ordained, the warriors
Divided into groups.

Through the scrub, traversing hills
And down towards the sea;
The burdened bods in separate line
Squelched through a sodden lea.

Pushing on a'fore their fate
In stealth and dawn's dim haze,
Each group awe-struck in suddenness...
It held their peering gaze.

Perceiving in the distant grey
An odd shape of great size;
Could easily be the hidey hole
Of the Father of All Lies!

Rising from the river's mouth
There loomed the darkest sight;
A fortress so formidable,
It climbed to endless height.

Shaped hugely like a Cygnus,
And causing all to cower;
The 'Black Swan's' neck all twisted 'round
To form a leaning tower.

Its wings spread out to form a block
To ocean's restless tide,
Facing t'wards the hills so bold;
It stood in taunting pride.

Cavaliere, his troops dispersed,
Now hidden in the bogs,
That formed a steaming barrier –
A maze with pea soup fogs.

Poised to risk all life and limb
And penetrate the maze;
This labyrinth of puzzlement
Once formed in ancient days.

And lurking in the 'Swan's' dim depths
In medieval swank;
Putrida in expectancy;
He opulently stank.

SCROLL THE ELEVENTH

The Day of Reckoning in the vicinity of their final destiny:
Wherein Manzana Putrida is humoured as
Cavalier and his troopers push
on into the shadow of the birdly demesne;
and unexpectantly meet
an unexpected stranger...

Sinking to their armpits
And oozing through the mud,
The troopers forged their way to doom
With leeches sucking blood.

Losing all direction
As they trod a tardy course,
Cavaliere gave orders
That each man discard his horse.

Silence poured out thickly
From that watchful, muted 'bird',
As the trekkers chose their passage
Through this ravelment absurd.

To the right and take a left,
Then sharply turn a corner,
Trusting that each move they made
Would lead them from this sauna.

Again confusion reigned supreme,
Again they'd lost their way,
Meandering in zigzags
As their nerves began to fray.

And peering from a turret high,
Putrida bit his knuckle;
For him the sport grew mischievous
And so began to chuckle.

More frustration loomed ahead
With each new thwarted chance,
To move ahead and up and out...
No further need to blanch.

Relieved, the parties finally reached
The point of no return.
Gladly rising from the sludge
That caused them grave concern.

Their garments covered head to toe
With sewage, waste and slop;
A moment to regain their poise
With new schemes to adopt.

Searching now for signs of life,
This fortress strangely bare
Of waiting guards or seneschal...
A rum ploy to declare.

Drawn as if by magnets
Towards the gaping gates;
A sense of bitter loneliness
Struck each, and all his mates.

With Cygnus towering overhead,
The noonday star above,
Cavaliere strode boldly to
The prison of his love.

His father dropping further back,
His presence now redundant;
Yet rather pray the deed be done,
Swift end...then Life Abundant.

The Younger though was unaware
Of moves behind the scenes,
Seeking routes to Adelade
By using any means.

Shadows rolling over all,
Passing through the portals;
Deeper towards the dungeon pyres –
Eternal dread of mortals.

Sinking further, rounding corners,
Still no opposition;
A chance to steal precious time,
Improving disposition.

Edging on from stone to stone
And clinging to the walls,
Cavaliere and friends could make out
Faintly searching calls.

In haste they stumbled to the source;
The murk waned dimmer still.
And lo, behold, before their eyes
A dungeon built to kill.

Sir Sedny, first to reach the door,
Thus through the bars did peer;
The sight that struck his innocence
Drew out a caring tear.

Trussed up tight as chicken wings,
A nervous wreck was bound.
He turned his head to face the knight –
Release at last is found!

"Sad grief, Dear Man, who brought you here
To this unending hell?
Destroy these bonds and exit, fast,
For there is much to tell."

Cavaliere, compassion huge
Towards this helpless creature,
Sought in vain to prise him out –
Impenetrable feature.

"It will not budge, this door of rock!
How can we get you out?
Tell us with what tricks at hand
We may acquire the clout."

Powerless it seemed to all
To free him from his pain.
Now truth extracted from this one –
Intelligence to gain.

"I, the Prince Cavaliere,
The Younger growing strong;
Speak up, My Man, prepare us now
To hear the silenced wrong."

Confusing thoughts and mixed emotions
Emanating to
The troops who stood with baited breath,
Waiting for the clue.

"Events of late, progressing forth
To denigrate my birth.
The sight you hold before your eyes...
None other than Lord Purth!"

"You're what? How dare you jest with us!
What do you think you're doing?
Get back, My Men, and draw your swords;
Take care the plot he's brewing!"

"No wait! You make a huge mistake,
Dismissing me as rotten.
Putrida now my name has snatched –
The fortress, too, ill-gotten.

"God knows how long I've been like this,
The stench too much to take.
There's now no time for you to lose
With many lives at stake!"

Suddenly a thunder's roar
From right, or was it left?
Heard above the victim's voice,
Clearly forged a cleft.

The fissure in the wall now plain
Behind the weary troops;
Sir Bell a'Rat stepped out towards
The unsuspecting dupes.

"A Ha! Sucked in again, My Friends.
I just don't think it's fair,
To see you suffer this much pain...
Stupidity seen bare!"

Needling Cavaliere,
He cut him to the quick,
And circled him with many guards;
Sir Sedny feeling sick.

"Vomit all you like, Pigdog,
There's nothing that can stop
Putrida's plans to join the Shields –
You goody-goody flop!

"Follow me, You Morons,
My Lord awaits his prey.
His beady eyes will fill with mist;
You're sure to make his day!"

Disarmed and badly beaten
By Sir Bell a'Rat's slick ploy,
The party followed meekly
To become Putrida's toy.

Leaving Purth behind them
Amidst his moans and groans,
The warriors trudged on in dread,
Expecting broken bones.

Through a steamy tunnel
And out into the gloom;
Shoved into a chamber
That signified their doom.

And straight ahead, before their eyes,
Stretched out upon the rack –
Dear Adelade, limbs tightly bound,
Bemoaned a breaking back.

Her golden locks revealed a face
Still transient in mind;
Albeit her beauty still intact –
But absolutely blind.

And overseeing Adelade
With raspy, heavy breathing,
Putrida stood with fellow louts
Whose lusts were hotly seething.

SCROLL THE TWELFTH

In the Depths of Degradation: Wherein
IT IS FINISHED!

Baldish skull and goatee
And fingers ringed with jewels;
The only things Putrida lacked
Were horns to scare the fools.

And to his left stood Melbun,
A hunchbacked little worm;
His voice in high falsetto
When he spoke to make all squirm.

"Bend your knees, You Sissies,
Behold and face the Law.
Bend your backs and buttocks
Or I'll go and fetch yon Cror!"

Cavaliere, not bound to be
A slave unto another,
Spoke up in bold defiance;
This Melbun's whine to smother.

"Desist, You Slimy Coward;
The writing's on the wall[6].
Before I bow my knee full stop,
Putrida I'll see fall!"

"Insolence! Gross insolence!"
Putrida e'er alert
For acts against his growing power;
His conversation curt.

"His Shield!" came the order;
Swiftly wrenched away.
Cavaliere was powerless 'fore
His enemy's foul play.

Putrida's tone now mocking:
"Where's your Daddypoo?
Your guileless geriatric
Gave up his little *coup*?"

Cavaliere turned quickly 'round –
His heart stopped with a thud:
"My Father! Why forsake me now,
My only flesh and blood?"

"Lonely, lonely little boy,"
Putrida slyly said.
"Pity he's not here to see
His little boy drop dead!"

"How dare you speak to him like that!"
Sir Sedny's voice so bold.
Putrida's piercing glare broke through;
Sedny's heart grew cold.

"Are you so brash, My Little Fop,
To speak to ME like that?
How dare you, Ugly Pus Head,
Wallow in your fat!"

Sedny, chest now thrusting out,
Spoke up in one last chance:
"Sir Ben Deego I slayed, forsooth;
He died by sword and lance!"

"You Silly Fool, you think you're brave
Because he died by you?
Ben Deego due to die at length –
Even if by flu!

"Deego held the Shield of Death –
His time was always up.
I knew of this before the man
Had even shared my cup.

"Knowing he would perish
At Sedny's clumsy hand,
I sent the Kiss of Death to YOU –
The bigger fish to land!

"Bell a'Rat, now do your job
Before the finished hour.
We meld this Shield to Golden Tree...
I have it in my power!"

Swiftly thus, the callous knight
Slid a lengthy dagger
Into Younger's heaving ribs...
Who then began to stagger.

His blood escaped in steady flows
To Cross out ugly crime;
Descended with his outstretched arms
Into Putrida's grime.

Laughing fits in mockery
At Ralia's darkest gloom:
"'Tis obvious my Cygnus
Has become your final tomb!"

A shriek broke from Dear Adelade
As she lay upon the rack!
And lightning struck the turrets
With a mighty, flashing crack!

Cavaliere screamed out in pain:
"Dear Father, here's your Son!
Send me to the deepest depths –
I'M DONE! IT'S DONE! YES, DONE!"

Cries of grief rose upwards
From the disbelieving party;
Putrida, Melbun, Bell a'Rat
Now snearing, ever hearty.

"He had to die, You Cretins!
He held the Shield of Sin.
Now I am the MASTER!"
From ear to ear his grin.

"Make way, You Fools, I join the Shields!
Behold, the Golden Tree!
I turn the wheel that brings them close!
How proud I am of me!"

The Shield of Life upon a frame
That sat upon a dais;
And opposite, the Silver Tree –
Its presence spewing chaos!

Putrida, maddened in his lust,
Began to turn the levers
That brought the Shields within a yard –
They danced, those eager beavers.

Closer still the Shields moved
T'ward the evil moment.
Could nothing stop the melding heat;
Their deadly deeds to foment?

Then from the heights of Cygnus,
Rotating t'wards the horde,
Aiming for the dais sparks -
A white-hot, flaming sword!

Whooshing through the atmosphere,
The sword came screaming in,
And wedged itself between the Shields
To thwart Eternal Sin!

Hurled off from the dais
By the glowing, pure heat,
Putrida fell upon the floor,
Then made it to his feet.

Hurtling down from turrets high,
Orlbry clenched his fist:
"Methinks your plans have gone astray!"
Putrida only hissed.

Orlbry's troops descended
To collect the scum and strays,
But Putrida, Melbun, Bell a'Rat
Escaped through tunnelways.

"After them, don't let them go!"
Cried Orlbry through the glare.
Then as his troops departed hence,
He saw Cavaliere.

"Too late, too late once more,
My Folks, We've been, alas, too slack.
O please, Dear God in hea'en above,
Bring this Younger back!"

Rushing to the dais,
He snatched the Golden Tree
And lay it 'pon Cavaliere:
"Bring him back for Thee!"

The eyelids of Cavaliere,
Once closed unto his end,
Opened now quite suddenly;
His legs began to bend.

Orlbry, shocked and shaken,
Spluttered words were spoken:
"Cavaliere! Alive again!
The curse at last is broken!"

Ascended strong Cavaliere
From death and its foul stink.
Cavaliere returned the Shield
And sealed the living link.

Younger Prince, now fully healed
Of wounds and hurts so deep,
Raced across to Adelade
To break her fatal sleep.

Not only blind, but dead unto
This life with all its woes;
Taken from her risen Liege –
Slain by HIS death-throes.

Rigor mortis setting in,
This deadly web had spun;
The Younger in vitality
Perceived HIS life had won!

He breathed upon her eyelids,
Then gave the Kiss of Life.
He cut the bonds that held her tight –
Now FREE...his lovely wife!

Beholding now each other's eyes,
Their cheeks in reddened blush;
He took her from her bondage
In prevailing holy hush.

EPILOGUE...

A new moon rises across the continent of Ralia: Wherein
The Prince returns with his Bride and victory is secured!

Riding from the sunset
Towards the eastern slopes,
Cavaliere and Adelade
Revived and quickened hopes.

The wedding bells resounding
Through this land so vast and spare;
The land once caught in bondage,
Now threw away its care.

The Marriage Feast so dearly sought
Will shine in overt glory;
The seal of hopes and ceaseless prayers...
The Climax of this Story!

Sir Sedny, Noah Lunga,
Grand Duke Orlbry, of course,
Returned with Prince Cavaliere
To herald a mighty force.

The hapless Purth, released at once
From hopelessness and dearth;
His name restored in honour
And his 'Swan' enjoys rebirth.

Putrida and his cohort,
From power they quickly fell;
Their trickery no more to fear –
Their end a living Hell.

Sir Bell a'Rat and Melbun
Eventually were caught;
Succumbed to loving grace and peace -
Redemption dearly bought.

Yet even though at times it seems
That wickedness prevails,
Do not forget the Flaming Sword;
It never, never fails!

With this the Words of God do speak
To us of Loving Grace;
The *Crux Eterna* formed the Way
To free our fallen Race.

Golden Tree prevailing
In the midst of fruitful soils,
Releasing us from all the ills
Of endless, worthless toils.

The Tree that with great bounty
Gives its Life to all with mercy,
'Til time determined by the King,
Must yield its Food here firstly.

The Shield of Life and Shield of Death,
No longer need for dread
Of being joined in darkest doom;
The threat forever dead.

The Shield of Life, still wedged away
From all that mischief gives;
Its power resides in Higher Realms
Where Father King still lives.

Hence His Life has come to us
With one repeated plea:
To liberate the native
And set the captive free.

To hold up high His Dignity,
To free the free from Pride;
Thus edify this continent;
And woo us all...the Bride!

THIS is the END of LOST RALIA!

NOTES

1. p. v   Refer to "The Chronicles of Narnia" by CS Lewis.

2. p. 16   Refer to "The Myths and Legends of King Arthur and the Knights of the Round Table" by Rick Wakeman.

3. p. 65   Now reverted to its indigenous name of 'Uluru'.

4. p. 86   Refer to Act 3, Scene 1 of "Hamlet" by William Shakespeare.

5. p. 98   Refer to "The Book of Judges" chapters 6 and 7.

6. p. 129   Refer to "The Book of Daniel" chapter 5.